A collection of short stories

by

MAMA

(with help from Robert Pearce)

Lots & Love,
Mama G
xx

The Very True Story of Mama G
by Freddie Whitehead, age 7, from Meopham, UK.

THE VERY TRUE STORY OF MAMA G

✻ ✻ ✻

Do you like fairytales?
Because my life is quite the fairy tale!

Have you ever heard of a lady called Mother Goose?
Well, she lived a long time ago in the seventeenth century.
And you'll never guess what?
She was me.
I was her.
We were we!

Originally I was from France.
Oui oui.
(But conveniently I've always sounded British.)
And I brought happiness to thousands and thousands of people, by telling stories.

I was the first person to tell some very famous stories.
You might have heard of them.
If you have: give me a cheer!
I was the first person to tell the story of:
Sleeping Beauty.
And *Little Red Riding Hood.*

And *Puss in Boots.*
And *Cinderella.*
And *Tom Thumb.*

Have you heard of them?
You have heard of them!
How marvellous!

I loved telling all these stories.
They made people happy, you know.
They made people realise that anything is possible.
And they made people realise that dreams can come true. Even for you.

But my success was making someone very jealous.
My good friend, Charles Perrault.
He was a storyteller too.
In fact, he helped me write a lot of my stories.
But nobody wanted to hear him read them out loud because he was such a grumpy old man.

One day this all got too much for him.
And he turned up at my cottage with a Custard Cream.
(That's a type of biscuit, that is.)
Apparently he'd been trying to find a Gypsy Queen, which would have made more sense in a fairytale, but given their nomadic nature and the fact that you shouldn't say gypsy anymore it had all become rather complicated.

"Eat the biscuit," he said.

"Oh, Charles, wouldn't you like to come in for a coffee first?"

"Non! You make your coffee like you make your words. The British way! And I will have neither in my mouth!"

"Oh. La. La." I thought.
And well, not wanting to be rude...
(I am a terribly polite lady, you see.)

4

...I took a bite of the biscuit.
Turns out. That was a mistake.
I see that now.
Did I learn nothing from Snow White?

I started to cough.
I felt my throat close.
I fell to the floor.
I saw stars in front of me.
"What is happening?" I screamed.

"Mwahahahahahahahahaha," he laughed. "Mwa-hahahahahahahahahaha!"

"Sorry. Are you just going to laugh or are you going to tell me what's going on?"

"Mwahahah... oh, mais oui. If I tell you what is happening the story can develop. Good idea.
"You are turning into a goose.
"A goose that will live eternally.
"But, you will never be able to tell another story ever again.
"Mwahahahaha."

And just like that he vanished.

Well, I had to have a look at myself.
So I waddled over to my salles de bains (that's bathroom in French, thank you.)
And I took a look at myself in the mirror.
And got the shock of my life.
He was right.
I was a goose.
I tried to call for help, but all I could do was honk.

"Honk. Honk. Honk."

And Charles was right about another thing:
I would live eternally.

She used to bicycle all around the city exploring its streets.
She might have got some streetcars too.
But that doesn't tend to go well in New Orleans.
So luckily: she cycled a lot.

Have you ever been to New Orleans?
It's a magical place.
And full of all sorts of wonderful people.
And Ellen was one of those people.
But not for long.

When Ellen was thirteen her mum and dad stopped getting along.
In fact, they divorced.
Very dramatic.
And Ellen and Betty moved to Atlanta. Texas.
Atlanta, Texas?
Not the first Atlanta you think of.
If you are, indeed, thinking of Atlantas at all.

Divorce is not a very nice time for any family.
And Ellen knew that her mum was unhappy.
So Ellen would try and make Betty laugh.
She would do funny dances.
And she would do funny laughs.
And she would be so funny that her mum would cry with laughter.
And then Ellen would copy that too and make her mum laugh even more.

Ellen realised that she could make people happy by being funny.
But when she was a grown-up she tried a lot of other things first.
She worked in a law firm.
She worked as a waitress.
She sold clothes.
And she painted houses.
But she realised that what she really wanted to do was make people laugh.

So? She made people laugh!

She performed at comedy clubs and made people laugh.
(And everyone knows that people who go to comedy clubs are the least likely people to laugh. In the whole wide world. Ever.)
But they laughed at Ellen (in a good way.)
(Yes, there is a bad way. And never let anyone laugh at you like that.)

Soon, so many people were laughing at Ellen (in the good way) that some important men in suits decided to give her a show on the TV.
They liked her so much they called the show *Ellen.*
This was in 1994.
In 1994 a lot of men thought that women weren't as good as them.
We know that's wrong, right?
So, for Ellen this was a BIG achievement.

People liked that the Ellen on telly was a bit crazy and just like them.
Then in 1997 something amazing happened:
The TV version of Ellen told Oprah (wow!) that she liked to kiss girls.
Then, at the same time in 1997, something even more amazing happened:
The real Ellen told the whole world that she liked to kiss girls!

A lot of people thought that this was brave.
But other people thought it was wrong and didn't like that Ellen wasn't as much like them as they thought.
People stopped watching her on the television.
And big companies stopped giving her money to talk about things they wanted to sell.
(And that's good. Sort of. Because you shouldn't support people who won't support you.)
And then her TV show was shut down.
All because she wanted to be who she was.

That was the sad bit.

Luckily, Ellen knew that what she had done was right.
She could tell because she had inspired lots of other men and women to do the same thing.
(Although, the men said they liked to kiss men.

If they'd said they liked to kiss girls that wouldn't have been as interesting.)

So, Ellen carried on trying to make people laugh and started to prove that who she chose to love didn't change who she was.

And people started to agree.

Phew.

She was in Finding Nemo.

Best. Film. Ever.

She had a talk show.

Best. Talk show. Ever.

She met lots of important and famous people.

Best. Oscars selfie. Ever.

And she showed us all that being true to you is the best way to be successful.

Best. Way to be successful. Ever.

And she got married.

To a girl called Portia.

And people didn't mind that Portia was a girl.

They wanted Ellen to be happy.

And Ellen Degeneres wants you to be happy too.

EUNICE THE HORSE

❋ ❋ ❋

Eunice the Horse.
Eunice the Horse?
That's a silly sounding name, isn't it?
It hardly canters off the tongue like Mickey Mouse, or Bugs Bunny, or Ryan Reynolds.
Let's just stop there.
Only for a moment.
To appreciate Ryan Reynolds.

But Eunice the Horse?
Come on! What a daft name!
And Eunice the Horse thought so too.

Because she knew she wasn't a horse.

I mean, she was a horse.
She'd been a horse since the day she was born.
She had horse parents.
And at the Happy Hill Farm she lived in a field full of other horses.

But Eunice knew she wasn't a horse.

She watched the other horses jumping over fences.
And she thought: "I won't jump. I'd much rather fly…"

She watched the other horses run around the paddock.

And she thought: "I won't run. They kick up dust. And I'd much rather kick up magic…"

Everywhere she stepped in the field she saw horse poop.
And she thought: "I won't poop. Not until I can poop glitter…"

You see, Eunice knew she wasn't like the other horses.
But what Eunice didn't know was what she was.
And this made her very, very sad.

One day, her best friend Hortense the Horse.
(Now that is an excellent name for a horse!)
Well, one day, Hortense decided that enough was enough.

"Come on Eunice," said Hortense. "Let's go and find your tribe."
"But we only know the other horses," whinnied Eunice.
"There's a whole world out there, Eunice, and I think it's time for you to explore it!"

So, Eunice took a leap of faith and jumped over the fence with Hortense.
They had barely landed before Hortense saw Eunice trotting off to investigate some large pink round objects that were playing in the mud.

"What are you?" asked Eunice.
"We're pigs!"
"Do you think I'm a pig?"
"Well, you don't look like one; but it's important not to judge someone just on the way they look."
"Can we try being pigs?" asked Hortense.
"Of course!"

So, the two horses climbed into the pig sty and did what pigs do:
The rolled around in the mud.
They oinked and grunted.
And they ate everything that was thrown at them.
After a while Eunice knew that being dirty all the time wasn't for her.

Eunice knew she wasn't a horse.
But she knew she wasn't a pig either.

They went to the next field.
"What are you?" asked Eunice.
"We're cows!"
"Do you think I'm a cow?"
"Well, you don't look like one; but everyone is unique, so who are we to judge?"
"Can we try being cows?" asked Hortense.
"Of course!"

So, the two horses went through the gate and did what cows do:
They ate grass.
They sat down when they thought it was going to rain.
And they farted so much they thought that they must be destroying the planet.
After a while Eunice knew that eating so much grass you had to fart all the time really wasn't for her.

Eunice knew she wasn't a horse.
But she knew she wasn't a cow either.

They went to the next field.
"What are you?" asked Eunice.
"We're sheep!"
"Do you think I'm a sheep?"
"Well, you don't look like one; but even mutton dress as lamb, so who are we to judge?"
"Can we try being sheep?" aked Hortense.
"Of course!"

So they went into the field and did what sheep do:
They got herded into another field by a dog.
They blindly followed the other sheep around.
And they panicked every time they smelled mint.
After a while Eunice realised that she was far too independent and being a sheep wasn't for her.

Eunice knew she wasn't a horse.
But she knew she wasn't a sheep either.

That night Eunice cried herself to sleep.
That night the sky was full of stars.
And as Eunice slept, the Northern Star shone the brightest and cast a magic spell over her.
That night Eunice's life changed forever.

When she woke up she felt different.
She knew who she was.
She knew what she was meant to be.
And she knew what she had to do.

She woke Hortense up.
"What is it?"
"I know what I am and I need you to help me make the changes!"
"What are you going to become?"
"I'm not sure what it is, but I know it's what I'm meant to be!"

The first thing Eunice needed was to be able to poop glitter and rainbows.
So, the two horses galloped down to the farm house.
Hortense did some reconnaissance to make sure no one was in.
And when she got the all clear Eunice knocked the door down and ransacked the house until she found the arts and crafts supplies.
Hortense was surprised to see her best friend chowing down on glitter like it was the finest hay.
But she knew not to question someone following their dreams.

Can you guess what Eunice is becoming?

The second thing Eunice needed was wings.
The two horses caused havoc in the chicken pen plucking the birds of their feathers.
But the chickens didn't put up too much of a fight.
Hortense was surprised to see Eunice sticking feathers onto her back with glue from the farmhouse.
But she knew not to question someone following their dreams.

Can you guess what Eunice is becoming?

The third thing Eunice needed was a horn.

Where would they get a horn from?

They looked all around, but there were no rhinoceros', antelopes or bisons on the farm.

Was this the end of Eunice's dream?

Then Hortense realised! "Turn that glue stick upside down!"

Hortense was still pretty surprised to see her friend put a glue stick on her head.

But she knew not to question someone following their dreams.

The transformation was complete.

"Eunice!" Screamed Hortense. "You're a unicorn!"

Eunice the Unicorn.

Now THAT sounds right.

Eunice the Unicorn flew around the farm.

The pigs oinked.

The cows mooed.

The sheep baaed.

And the chickens, despite now being completely naked, were proud.

Proud to have helped someone become fabulous.

Proud to have helped someone become one of a kind.

Proud to have helped someone become themselves.

Eunice was a unicorn.

And from that day she never looked back.

Apart from when she farted glitter.

That was always worth looking back for.

Cinder-Fella
by Pepper, age 5, from crystal Palace,UK

CINDER-FELLA

* * *

Sammy was watching the rain through the window.
Sammy was listening to Celine Dion power ballads.
Sammy was pretending he was Rachel in *Friends* after she realised her and Ross weren't just 'on a break'.
(You've not seen it? Netflix. Now. I'll wait.)
Sammy was feeling sad.

A few months ago, Sammy's mum had got very poorly.
In a matter of weeks, she had passed away.
And today had been her funeral.
That's why Sammy was sad.

And to make matters worse: now he was on his way to live with his Uncle Donald and his two cousins, Margaret and Theresa.
Sammy did not have a good feeling about this.
At all.
Not at all at all.
At all.
At. All.
At.
All.

Celine Dion stopped.

So did the car.
The rain didn't.

Sammy stepped into the rain and rang his Uncle's doorbell.
And waited.
And got wet.

What was worse is that he could hear Margaret and Theresa laughing on the other side of the door.
"Let's not let him in," said Margaret.
"There's nothing for him here," replied Theresa.
They laughed some more.

This was typical them.
So long as they were okay, they weren't worried about anybody else.

Eventually Uncle Donald called down.
"If you want to get in you'll have to climb over the wall and come through the back."

It was a high wall.
Sammy couldn't get him and his bag up and over it.
So, he had to make a difficult decision: he left his possessions on the street, in the rain and climbed over into his Uncle's garden.
What else could he do? He was desperate.

Margaret and Theresa were waiting for him in the kitchen.
Their faces were contorted into insincere smiles.
They looked so silly!

"The prince is holding one of his balls," said Margaret.
"And we're going," said Theresa.
(Who had been practicing her curtsies for years, just for this occasion. You should see them, she can go really low. It's very impressive. But also, weird.)

"But you're not invited," said Uncle Donald escorting his daughter's out the door.
"That's a shame," thought Sammy. "I think balls may be just my thing."

Sammy started to feel sad again.
He watched the rain through the window. Again.
He listened to Celine Dion power ballads. Again.
He pretended he was Rachel in...
NO!
Before he even got to split up with Ross, Sammy had a bright idea!

"I'm going to go to the ball and meet the Prince. Just like Cinderella!"
Except Sammy was going to have to be his own Fairy Godmother.
A Fairy Sammymother, if you will.
But you won't.

Sammy was about to leave the house when he realised one thing.
If he went to the ball in what he was wearing his family would recognise him right away.
He would have to change.
Into a disguise.
Sammy thought about this for a while.
And then a lightbulb flashed above his head.
Either Sammy had just had a good idea, or the electricity was faulty.
The lightbulb stayed on.
Fantastic!
He'd had a good idea!

He dashed up to his cousins' closets.
He rifled through their draws.
(No one had done that for a long time.)

He put on everything that he could find.
And ended up in a bright purple skirt.
A yellow top.
And a pair of crocs.

Sammy was ready to meet a prince.

Sammy knew this was going to be the best night of his life.

The palace ballroom was an explosion of colour, glitter and sparkle.
Fairy lights hung everywhere.

People were chatting and people were dancing and a band was playing on the balcony.

From the top of the grand staircase Sammy could see Margaret and Theresa scaring men off left and right (but mostly left.)
Sammy couldn't help but laugh!
They had no idea he was there!

Then Sammy saw him.
The Prince.
Prince Charming.
He was the most perfect person anyone had ever seen.
Sammy felt his knees give way.
And he fainted.
Like any good damsel in distress does.

When Sammy came to, he could hear Margaret and Theresa arguing with someone.
"That princess looks too poor. We can't help her. What can she do for us?" said Theresa.
"Really she should start by helping herself," said Margaret.

"You must be the worst people I have ever met!"
Could it be?
Prince Charming was standing up for him.
Her.
Sammy was in disguise.
It's important we don't forget that.

The Prince helped Sammy up.
"Would you care for a dance?" he asked.
Sammy nodded.
And that was that.
They danced all night.
And looked into each other's eyes.
You could say it was romantic.
But. Yuck.

When they weren't dancing they talked.

About music. And movies. And food. And Sammy's mum. And hopes. And dreams. And the Kardashians. And Sammy's mum.

Before too long Sammy noticed his uncle and cousins were leaving. Disaster!
He would have to get home before them if he didn't want to get found out.
He had no choice!
He pulled his gaze away from the prince.
He turned his head slowly to face the door.
And then. He legged it.
Leaving the prince empty handed and considerably confused.

Sammy got back to his Uncle's house in plenty of time.
He put his cousin's clothes back in their drawers.
And went to bed.
He had made quick progress compared to Donald, Margaret and Theresa.
But then, progress had never really been their thing.

The next morning everything was calm in the house.
Then.
"AAAAAAAARRRRRRRGGGGGGGGGHHHHHHHHHH".
Theresa had just seen the news and let out an excited cry.

What she had just read was that Prince Charming had fallen in love at his ball.
With a girl.
But he didn't know who the girl was.
And this morning the prince had decided that he was going to find this girl, no matter what it took.

The house was in disarray.
Margaret and Theresa had both realised that this might be their chance to be one of the most important women in the country. And boy, were they prepared to do anything for it.

And then. The doorbell rang.
No one moved.

The doorbell rang again.
Sammy went downstairs in his pyjamas and opened the door.

Before him stood Prince Charming.
Before Prince Charming stood Sammy.
They looked at each other.
They looked straight into each other's eyes.

"It's you!" said the Prince.
"It is." said Sammy.
"But you're a boy," said the Prince.
"I am," said Sammy.

Theresa looked aghast. "But I thought you'd fallen in love with a girl."
"And so did I," said the Prince. "But love is love. And I see my love in his eyes. The only thing is: I don't know your name."

The Prince looked at Sammy. "I suppose your name must be Cinder-Fella."
And from that moment, that's how Sammy was known.

And that's the end.
Well, not quite the end.
Sammy and Prince Charming lived a long and happy life together.
They adopted lots and lots of lovely children.
And their balls became famous around the world.
Thanks to the internet.

Margaret, Theresa and Uncle Donald went on to have some success too.
But they weren't for everyone. Despite what they thought.
And neither will this story be.
But I hope you liked it.

The Fairies Fran and Vera: Boy Oh Boy
by Samuel Wright, age 7, from Manchester, UK

THE FAIRIES FRAN AND VERA: BOY OH BOY

✻ ✻ ✻

Fabulous Fran was a fairy. Vile Vera was one too.
They lived together in Fairy Land; where dreams seem to come true.

Fabulous Fran does good things: she loves to make you smile.
While Vera has her wicked ways; that's why we call her Vile.

Good things come in many forms, like deeds and open hearts.
And Fran knew this very well, you see she was *fairy* smart.

But Vile Vera thought differently, she wanted the world to be bad.
She wanted it full of hate not love and wanted to make us mad.

"Coffee?" asked Vera at breakfast.
"Don't mind if I do," said Fran. "And what have you got to do today?"
"Oh, I've got a plan!"

"A plan?" said Fran. "That can't be good, what are you up to Vera?"
The coffee poured, our villain implored, that Fran move a little nearer.

"You know Silly Billy, whose address is: The Fairlawns, Fairy Land?
"He told me something the other day I'm struggling to understand.

"He's fallen in love."

"What's wrong with that?" said Fran, bubbling over with joy.
"Here's the fact: my problem's that he's fallen in love with a boy."

"A boy? Oh boy! That's wonderful!"
Fran had longed to hear news like this for years.
"But," said Vera with a tut. "I'm going to make this end in tears.

"Everyone knows that love is for a boy and girl to share,
"And by the end of the day, if I have my way, of this fact he'll be well aware.

"With a wave of my wand, Billy should see just what his life could be.
So, Vera gave a quick curse and Billy landed face first, amongst their jam and coffee.

Fran screamed. Vera laughed. Silly Billy's face was in the butter.
"Now to find you the perfect girl." Not words you want Vera to utter.

A fanfare played and in a glitter haze Milly came into their life.
"She's pretty," said Billy,
"Yes I am. And I'd be the perfect wife.
"When it comes to looks I'm by the books."
Billy said, "That can't be disputed."
"And what about you, you're handsome too!" Milly thought she and he were well suited.

But they weren't. For one reason. Do you know why?
"You'd be my perfect wife, Milly. If only you were a guy."

And as quick as you like, Milly vanished away, in a puff of smoke.
"Ooh," said Fran, "I tell you what: I can't wait to meet your bloke!"

But Vile Vera's villainous ways continued with spells and drama.
Until there appeared (and they were amazed) a furry, friendly, Llama!

"Have you lost your mind?" said Fran, kindly offering the llama some tea.
Then through the door crash Lily.
"Don't worry she's with me!"

"I'm a llama farmer and this one escaped. Oh, she's got a mind of her

own.
"Mind you, so have I, they say, that's why I live alone."

Then to the llama's alarm she was in Lily's arms and being taken out of the house.
Lily made the llama look so light you thought the llama might have been a mouse!

"Now there's a woman: strong and tough! Fran, don't you agree?"
"I do," said Fran.
But Billy sighed. "She's still not man enough for me."

"Third time lucky!" Vera cried, as Fran saw one of her worst fears:
Vile Vera was getting so angry steam was coming out her ears!

Her face went red, her blood was boiling and then before they knew it.
She flew into a thousand pieces. "Oh look," said Fran. "She blew it."

The pieces fell back in to place and this they thought was strange.
Instead of seeing Vera's face they saw her rearranged.

"What the what?" Billy exclaimed and Fran did much the same.
"Are you alright Vera dear? If indeed Vera's still your name!"

"Of course it's not. I'm now called Dot! Do you think you'd get along with me?"
"Well," said Billy. "I've always thought: I could be a friend of Dorothy's."

Dot looked at Fran askance and frankly Billy wondered why.
"Is that all I am to him?" she said. "A friend? I may just cry!"

And so the waterworks began! Tears poured forth from Dot's face.
"I'm very clever, you see, I have a degree, in gender politics and race."

Fran got a hanky and dabbed Dot's eyes and said: "Gosh, you are very smart.
"But not enough to know why you've not got Billy's heart."

And Dot howled and Dot wailed and her tears became a river,
Until Dot washed herself away and all that was left was Vera.

"Enough's enough," said Fran. "I have to intervene.
"Forcing someone to be something they're not is very, very mean.

"Billy is a good boy and he loves a good boy too.
"And honestly, Vera, who Billy loves isn't up to you."

"Oh yes it is!" said Vera, shooting her wand at Fran.
"Oh no it's not!" said Fran, shooting her wand right back.
"Is!"
"Isn't!"
"Is!"
"Isn't!"
They were both under attack.

Billy stood there eyes agog and gob down to the floor.
Sparks were flying around the room. Who knew what was in store?

Then there was a crash and then a flash and then a silence fell.
Between them the fairies had magicked a man. A man Billy knew quite well!

He was holding *The Complete Works of Shakespeare*. To Fran that was clever and strong.
While Vera just said: "He's pretty." And she pretty well wasn't wrong!

Billy's eyes were wider than ever and his smile was from ear to ear.
"Sam, my love, it's good to see you; I'm really glad you're here!"

They hugged, held hands and beamed with pride and for the first time Vera got it:
Love should never have to hide and no one has the right to stop it.

"Well, I suppose that's one more at the table for tea."
Said Fran.
Fabulously.

#PASSTHEPASTY

✻ ✻ ✻

I am a pasty.
Not a pastry.
A pasty.
In fact, I am a Cornish pasty.
And therefore, pasties do not come any better than me.

I look amazing.
I smell incredible.
I am legend.
Actually,
I.
Am.
Pasty.

So, you can imagine my surprise when I was kicking back on a baking tray with me other pasty peeps, when I heard on the radio that there's this woman in Scotland what's never had a bloomin' pasty.
I don't mean, like, not tried a Cornish pasty.
She has never had a single pasty past her lips in her actual whole entire life.
If you can call it a life.
I don't know how some people live. I really don't.

Well, I'm not a normal pasty, see.
As you can probably tell by the conversation we're having.

And if you think this is normal, for a pasty to be talking to you, you know, I think you should go and speak to someone about it.

And not a pasty this time.

A person.

Speak to a person.

Please.

Anyway, I thought, there and then, I thought "I've got to sort this out.

"This woman has gots to try a pasty!"

And that's not a normal thing to do.

Most pasties would just sit there.

Well, I said: "Fellas, you gotta get me off this baking tray, I gotta get to Scotland."

They said: "You can't."

I said: "I got to. There's a woman in this world not had a pasty."

The next thing I did was I called the radio.

Now stop thinking right now that a pasty could never use a telephone and call the radio station.

'Coz I can tell you that if you're going to come into this with that attitude then the rest of the story's gonna be very had to stomach.

And us pasties are not in the business of being hard to swallow.

And besides when you've got a passion for something you can achieve anything.

That's what my dear old mother told me and she fed the royals.

#SoProud

Now then, the radio took a little bit of convincing but eventually I was put through to this human called Greg James and I said: "Alls you got to do my darlin', is make sure that there are people in this beautiful country of ours that can get me from Padstow here in Cornwall to Newmacchar up there in Scotland.

"In one piece.

"It's imperative that I'm in one piece.

"People eat with their eyes see. And I need this lady to see me in my full perfection."

So, this Greg.

He asks the people listening to his show and they say: "Of course we'll help."

And before you know it #PassThePasty is trending on this thing called Twitter and I'm a sensation in my own life time.

I mean, I always knew I was different to the rest of them.

But I thought it was just the wholewheat flour.

How wrong was I?

First thing, I was going to get a ferry.

But first thing before that: I had to get out the bakery.

Now, it always gets very hot in this kitchen, because, well, we pasties are hot stuff. So, I happened to be next to an open window.

I said: "Lads, I gotta get out through that there hole in the wall."

So Old Pete (he was the first one to be made.) Old Pete shuffled himself off the tray and tucked himself under it so the whole thing sloped. And well, I slipped right off and straight out the window.

Big Barry had to stop the others doing the same.

We called him Big on account of his size, see, he was one of those extra-large pasties, so I knew he got this. And he did.

Good lad that Barry.

So, I'm out the window and I lands on an ants nest, but rather than let them get cross with me I had a calming word and they carried me all the way to the ferry, where this big human fella picked me up and put me in a box.

And I set sail.

The first pasty to captain a ferry.

That last bit's a joke.

I'm not the first.

But where was I going?

Well, as it so happens: Devon.

And this is where I found out that folk from Devon sound just like folk from Cornwall, but they do not like it if you tell them that.

And anyway, also as well: they do not like it if you tell them how to do their cream teas.

But who am I to get involved with all that nonsense?

I'm just a Cornish pasty who knows that if you put the cream on the scone before the jam then you're an absolute heathen who should be sent to a correctional facility.

People get right chewed up about some things, don't they?

But thank that great baker in the sky they didn't chew me up about it.

Besides, I was in a box; so I was totally safe.

But have you ever been in a box that's balanced on the back of a pedal bike?

I can tell you off of my first-hand experience that it is terrifying!

I thought I was gonna be a gonner on the A38.

You see, what happened was: I got off the ferry and was handed to this fella wearing lycra.

I thought: "Hello, he's got enough meat and veg for the two of us, he has."

Turns out, he was a cyclist on the Tour of Britain.

And he cycled me all the way to Bristol.

When I got there it turned out that the folk from there sounded a little bit like the folk from Cornwall and Devon, except they have this thing called a babber.

I never worked out what that was.

I assume they're all just big fans of that cartoon elephant off of the 1990s.

Like a lot of people: I didn't hang around in Bristol for long.

I got put in a car and I made my way to the Midlands.

That's the middle of the country, so I'm making good progress.

I almost wasn't though.

I must have been making the driver feel hungry, so she got out to get some food and left me to look after the keys.

Wait.

That doesn't make much sense.

She left a pasty to look after her keys?

Well, she realised too late.
I saw her turn back in panic.
I saw her try the car door.
It was locked, my darlings.
Had she just ruined everything?
And oh my great baker in the sky it was hot in there!
I swear I started to cook!

But nobody panic!
I was saved!

I'd say my bacon was saved, but I don't have any bacon in me.
And the good news is I was still as uncooked as they day I was born!
Oh and she cried.
It broke my little crust it did.
But I had to tell her, I said: "Darlin' don't be cryin' over me. This pastry is perfectly seasoned, it does not need anymore salt."

And you know what?
From that moment I thought: "You know what pasty? Not every pasty is as lucky as you are to get to see the world. It's time you had some adventures. You only live once. YOLO. Or in my case: POLO; pasties only live once.
And adventures I had my darlings.

I went to Tamworth. And no, Tamworth wasn't the adventure. Despite what you may think.
I went down a ski slope.
Hands free.
Which is quite easy for a pasty to do actually.

I went on a rollercoaster.
Now that was scary!
I swear the mince and onions nearly shot right of me!

And I went to Burnley Football Club's ground and almost got served at half-time.
Well, I had to get out of there as fast as I could.

And do you know? A friendly vegan smuggled me out.
If she couldn't eat me no one was going to eat me.

We didn't know where to go.
We didn't know what to do.
And then she realised.
I was going to Scotland!
And there's only one way to do that, according to her: by train.
Not by any old train, though.
Just an old one.
The Flying Scotsman.
The train to end all trains.
Oh, it was beautiful you shoulda seen it.
All red velvet.
A luxurious trolley service.
I could have stayed on there for days.
There was just one tiny problem.
It was not going to Scotland.
Stupid name for a train then, in't it.
Scotsman.

But I got this far and I wasn't going to let a tiny problem like that get in my way.
Usually the biggest problem we pasties face is too much potato not enough meat.
But this! This was different!
Oh I was living!
I felt like the James Bond of pasties, I did!
But what was I gonna do?

Well, I spoke to the train guard.
And I asked him how good his throw was.
And whether his aim was alright.
He said they weren't half bad, either of them.
So we forged ahead with a plan.

Turns out there's a stretch of railway that goes alongside a motorway.

We both sat by the window.
The train guard and me.
Waiting for a truck to come by and align with the train.
We didn't know how long this road and rail situation was going to last, so we had to be quick.

A truck turned up.
The guard got him to wind his window down.
We both took a deep breath and the train guard hurled me through the air towards the truck.
It was so liberating!
The wind in my crust.
The lovely countryside below.
The birds looking so confused.

I landed on the passenger seat of the truck.
The driver looked at me and said: "Where to mate?"
And I said: "Scotland. They may take our lives, but they will never take our freedom!"
Then we just sat there in silence for quite a few hours.
He'd never seen *Braveheart*.
So I'd just made a pretty bold statement for a pasty.

We crossed the border in triumph!
Then we rolled back a bit so we could have our picture taken with the 'Welcome to Scotland' sign.
And it's there the trucker told me that this was as far as we could go together.
I was so close and yet still so far.

I've never done this in my life.
Why I would I have? I'm a pasty.
But I had to resort to hitchhiking, my darlin's.
I'm not a proud pasty, me.
I'm proud of being a pasty.
Now that's true.

Well, this car pulled up.

And this girl got out.
And she couldn't believe what she was seeing.
She screamed. She was hysterical. She couldn't get her words out.
I could tell. To her I was the Tom Cruise of the pasty world.
(I'm small and I do all my own stunts.)
And she knew where I was going.
She'd been following this whole thing on the radio.
She knelt down to me.
Looked me straight in the steam holes and said: "Will you do me the honour of letting me take you to your destination?"

How could I refuse?
She picked me up, so gently, in her arms and put me in her car.
And then we drove.
And drove.
And drove.
Scotland is way bigger than you think it is.

And then we arrived.
You shoulda seen it! It was quite the ceremony.
We parked around the corner from where this woman's house was.
We were greeted by two soldiers and a man blowing wind through a bag and out some pipes.
I thought he was professional hyperventilator.
But no, he was a musician.
And the bagpipes are a thing.
I have learnt so much.

We went round the corner and there was such a big crowd.
All the neighbours were out.
There were cameras and microphones everywhere.
And when they saw me they all cheered!
And quite rightly.
For I.
Am.
Pasty.

I got handed over to the woman what had started all this.

And amongst all the cheering and excitement…

We had to wait for twenty-seven minutes whilst I got cooked.

Hello everybody.
Mama G here.
I've got to take over the story at this point…
For reasons that will become clear.

Well they waited twenty-seven minutes.

…

…

…

The BBC even let Greg James keep his show on the air for longer than it should have been so his listeners could hear this lovely lady, Sarah she was called, take her first bite of pasty.
And I think she liked it as much as the rest of us do; although I did see her plate and she left quite a lot, which is not something I've ever experienced when it comes to pasties.

And you see, once a pasty's been eaten, it's hard for it to carry on talking.
It's almost like its job here is done.
But what a job our little pasty friend did this time!
He knew he was worth the effort.
And so did the rest of the country.

And you know what?
You're worth the effort too!

I just hope you don't get eaten.

EVERYBODY SAY LOVE

✳ ✳ ✳

When I say "love", you say "love".
Love. **(Love.)**
Love. **(Love.)**
That's it! Everybody say "love." **(Love.)**

Everybody Say Love (Love) was a massive hit for our star Love Llewellyn.
It was a one hit wonder, of course, but Love didn't care; because with that one hit she had done something wonderful.
As you'll find out.
If you'll just let me carry on with the story.
Gosh.

But I can't carry on with the story until I've introduced you to the lady herself: Love Llewellyn.

Love is Welsh.
Which is weird.
Because I can't do a Welsh accent. And I wrote the story. And I'm going to have to do a Welsh accent.
I can do a Yorkshire accent.
But you never heard of anyone with the surname Llewellyn coming from Yorkshire, did you?
But that's a stereotype.

And I'm here to breakdown stereotypes.
So, Love Llewellyn was from Yorkshire.
That's that sorted.

But there's a lot more to Love than just where she came from.

Love is gay.
Love is black.
Love is blind.
Love is love is love is love is love is love etc.
You get the point.

Love is also a word.
Love is a magical, special word that can make your heart soar.
It's a word that everyone deserves to hear.
And it's a feeling that everyone deserves to feel.

But Love Llewellyn only knew that Love was her name.
And this is a story of how Love Llewellyn used her name to get the love that she deserved.

Before I continue there's just one thing I need to double check with you.
When I say "love", you say "love".
Love. **(Love.)**
Love. **(Love.)**
That's it! Everybody say "love." **(Love.)**

Love was born black.
This will come as no surprise to you because you know that people are born all sorts of different colours.
Sometimes it's to do with their cultural heritage.
And sometimes it's a medical emergency.
But in the case of Love Llewellyn it was her heritage.
Her parents had been born black too, you see.

And this was a bit much for the little village that Love Llewellyn grew up in.
They weren't used to people being born black there.
They called her all sorts of names.

They called her darky.
They called her Sambo.
They called her pickaninny.
And some even worse words that I never want to hear people being called.

One day Love Llewellyn stopped them.
She took a deep breath and said.
In a Yorkshire accent.
"If you're going to call me any name, call me by my name.
"My name is Love.
"Everybody say 'love,' **(Love.)**
"Everybody say 'love.'" **(Love.)**

Now, you know the saying "love is blind," don't you?
Well, Love Llewellyn took this very literally.
For Love Llewellyn was blind.
In the eyes.
She couldn't see a thing.
And this was another thing people would call her names for.
They called her cretin.
They called her loser.
They called her freak.
And some even worse words that I never want to hear people being called.

One day Love Llewellyn stopped them.
She took a deep breath and said.
"If you're going to call me any name, call me by my name.
"My name is Love.
"Everybody say 'love,' **(Love.)**
"Everybody say 'love.'" **(Love.)**

You've probably guessed that growing up wasn't very easy for Love Llewyellen.
But she took solace in some wonderful things; as you do when times are hard.
She loved retro prison dramas. #PrisonerCellBlockH

She obsessed over Ariana Grande.

And she loved listening to audio descriptions of Serena Willams at Wimbledon.

I don't know about you.

But I think that Love Llewellyn may have been gay.

I'm not the only one who thinks that.

Love Llewellyn thought that too.

And so did the rest of the village.

And you'll never guess what. They called her names.

They called her queer.

They called her lezzer.

They called her butch.

And some even worse words that I never want to hear people being called.

One day Love Llewellyn stopped them.

She took a deep breath and said.

"If you're going to call me any name, call me by my name.

"My name is Love.

"Everybody say 'love,' **(Love.)**

"Everybody say 'love.'" **(Love.)**

Now, I'm curious.

What do you do when people are mean to you?

I eat...

Chocolate, crisps, anything.

In fact, sometimes it's got so bad that the corner shop next to my house has recently changed its name to 'Mama G's Sad Store!'

But I digress...

This isn't therapy.

But it's working.

Love Llewellyn cared about her waistline much more than I care about mine.

And when she got tired of being called names she wrote songs.

Oh! And they were good songs!

Songs about how she wanted to be called by her name.

Love.
And songs about how she wanted people to say the word "love" and to mean it.

And I think you know how one of her songs went.
When I say "love", you say "love".
Love. **(Love.)**
Love. **(Love.)**
That's it! Everybody say "love." **(Love.)**

It turned out that lots of people felt the same way as Love Llewellyn.
Her song *Everybody Say Love (Love)* became an international sensation.
Love Llewellyn became a huge star.
Everybody loved her.

And then she realised.
She had always been loved.
By her family.
By her friends.
And by her teachers.
She had just allowed her bullies voices to be the voices that she listened to.

And I want you to remember:
You are loved too.
Every single one of you.
By your families.
By your friends.
And by your teachers (so long as you're good in their classes!)

And I don't want you to ever forget that.

And if anyone tries to call you names just remember what Love Llewellyn did:
Say it with me.
Everybody say Love. **(Love.)**

Everybody. Say. Love.

The Worst Twitch
by Marnie Pearce, age 2, from Leicester, UK

THE WORST TWITCH

❋ ❋ ❋

"Vell, vell, vell, everybody; here ve are again at ze conference for ze vicked vitches. Are you all veeling vicked?"

"Yasssssss," shouted back all the vitches. Sorry. Witches.

I bet you were starting to wonder what this story was about, weren't you?

When I say everybody...
There was one witch who didn't "yassss."
In fact, she buried her head in her hands,
And said very quietly: "Noooooo."

You see, Willy the Witch...
(Willy's short for Wilhelmina.)
Well, Willy was just really good.
She couldn't help it.
And when you're a good witch, you're actually a very bad witch.

She'd been born into a long line of wicked witches and evil enchanters.
And despite her best efforts to fit in she just couldn't help being good.

But you'll never guess what?
The rest of her family hadn't noticed!
They thought she was just like the rest of them.
They even had the audacity to describe her as normal.
As if being wicked and evil is normal.

But then let's face it: it's not.
Nothing is.
None of us are normal!

Willy did a good job of not sticking out.
But there was one thing that kept almost giving her away.
Her twitch.

Whenever she had to serve very wicked witch she would get so nervous that her eye would spasm and blink.
And whatever bad thing she was trying to do.
Would end up being good.
As far as Willy could see it was the worst twitch.

And now, with her head in her hands she was thinking of all the times she'd been good.
Without meaning to be.

There'd been the time when Freddy (the boy at school she well fancied) didn't even look at her because he couldn't take his eyes off Gladys, the new girl.
Willy did everything she could to get his attention. But it didn't work.
She got so angry she decided she was going to turn him into a frog.
She thought mean things.
She said mean things.
And she waved her wand in a really angry way.
But wait.
What's happening?
Too late!
She twitched.
Rather than cast a mean spell her twitch made her cast a love spell.
And from that moment Freddy and Gladys have been hopelessly in love.

Then there'd been the time when she asked her dad what was for dinner.
And he said: "Cauldron Soup."
They had Cauldron Soup all the time.

Have you ever had Cauldron Soup?

I wouldn't recommend it.

It's full of snake, newt, frog, bat, dog, worm, lizard and owl.

Willy refused to eat it one more time.

She got so angry she decided to make the ingredients run riot all over the house!

She thought mean things.

She said mean things.

And she waved her wand in a really angry way.

But wait.

What's happening?

Too late!

She twitched.

Rather than cast a mean spell her twitch made her cast a benevolent spell.

And instead of a disgusting soup, Gordon Ramsey appeared and made them the most delicious soup they had ever tasted.

Then there'd been the time when Lucinda (the mean girl in her school) called Willy ugly.

And then went on to say some even worse things!

Lucinda said that Willy had warts.

That Willy smelled.

And that Willy's skin was a really weird shade of green.

Willy wasn't going to stand for this!

She got so angry she decided to make Lucinda as ugly as she could.

She thought mean things.

She said mean things.

And she waved her wand in a really angry way.

But wait.

What's happening?

Too late!

She twitched.

Rather than cast an ugly spell her twitch made her cast a beauty spell. And now Lucinda is recognised as the most beautiful woman in the whole entire world. Bar none.

Back to the Wicked Witch conference.
"Vitches! Let me hear you scream. Are you feeling vicked?"
"Yassssss!" Thousands of witches screamed again.
Willy stood up.
Everyone stopped "yasssssssss-ing."
Every witch in the room watched Willy rise.

"Vhat?"

"I need to tell you something."

Willy's mum held Willy's dad by the hands.
What was about to happen?

"VHAT?"

"It's just that. Um."

Willy's brothers and sisters all giggled into their hands. This was getting awkward.

"Vhat Villy? Vhat?!"

"I've known this for a long time. And maybe I should have said something sooner. It's just that. I'm not wicked."

Everyone took a sharp breath.
You could have heard a pin drop.

"I'm a good witch."

Well, the place went crazy.
Her mum started wailing.
Witches were laughing and pointing at her.
Witches were calling her horrible names.
Witches were sending spells in her direction to make her bad.

This is exactly why Willy hadn't wanted to tell anyone.
She knew no one would understand.
She was starting to get angry.
She wanted them all to just disappear and leave her alone.

She wanted to cast a mean spell on them all.
But wait.
Nothing was happening.
It was going to be too late.
She wasn't twitching.

And then she realised.

She didn't need to.
She didn't need to hide anything now.
She could be who she was.
And she was going to embrace it.

So, she cast a good spell.

"Double, double, toil and trouble,
Make them kind and break this bubble.
Cool it with the mean they should,
Then they'll love that I am good."

(That's almost Shakespeare that was. I hope you're impressed!)

Time stood still for a moment.

Willy took a deep breath.

Then.

Her mum's wailing became tears of joy.
Witches were cheering and shaking her hand.
Witches were chanting her name.
Witches were sending spells in her direction to make her know that she
was loved.

Her good spell had worked.
And now she could finally be who she had always been all along.
And that was good.

You might need to do a spell one day.
But I hope not.
Because everybody already knows you're wonderful as you are.

Mama G

And that's very good.

Swit Swoo Swan
by Henry Idle, age 5, from Auckland, New Zealand.

SWIT SWOO SWAN

❋ ❋ ❋

This is a true story.
Like, it actually happened.
This isn't any of your Hans Christian Anderson fan fiction.
No.
This is real life.

You are about to meet a goose and a swan and discover the greatest romance of our time.
Well, I say greatest.
Of course, it's no Jack and Rose, or Romeo and Juliet, or Gemma Collins and Gemma Collins.
But it is romance.
Pure and simple.
And that's not even Hear'Say.

Anyway, shall I begin?
It really is an egg-cellent story.

Picture it. New Zealand. A lake. 1977.
The whole lake is rocking out to the sound of, Seaweed Mac, Aquasmith and Iggy Pond.
And in the middle of all this rocking a mother goose is rocking. Back and forth. Laying egg, after egg, after egg.
So many eggs in fact that she's beginning to wish she'd never met the father goose.

Their eyes had met across a crowded pond.
He'd taken her out for dinner and picked up the bill.
She'd led him on a wild goose chase and been stuck with him ever since.
Geese mate for life, you see.

What a wonderfully ordinary family they'd been.
Two committed parents and five new goslings every year.
Then Thomas was born.

Thomas was a little different to his brothers and sisters.
He was the black sheep of the family.
Except he was white and a goose.

Thomas never wanted to go diving and racing with his father and brothers.
Instead he preferred to practice the elegant art of synchronised swimming with his mother and sisters.

Thomas never wanted to play with the boisterous Canada Geese.
Instead he preferred to gossip with the matriarchal swans as they swanned along their way.

Thomas never wanted to hang out with girl goslings, unless it was to shake a tail feather.
Instead he preferred to hang out with boy goslings; but if they were too nice he would get shy and waddle away.

Nobody knew what to make of Thomas.
Especially not father goose.
He would often be found down the local watering hole laughing and telling jokes at his son's expense.
But Thomas didn't mind.
How does the saying go?
"Water off a duck's back."
Oh. Except Thomas was a goose.
So actually: he did mind. A little bit.

He started to swim around by himself.

And tried to work out how he could be like everyone else.
But all he did was watch his brothers and sisters fall in love with other geese and have gaggles of goslings to care for.
Thomas had no one.
Thomas was very lonely.

That is until the 80s kicked in.
The whole lake was rocking out to the sound of Lily Idol, Frogette and 4 Newt Blondes,
When the rocking was interrupted by a squawking bevy of swans landing on the lake.

This is when Thomas met Henry.
This is when Thomas stopped being lonely.

Thomas had always liked swans.
But this time he REALLY liked swans.
Like, like liked.

Henry was just Thomas's type.
He was big.
And black.
And landed on the lake like he owned it.
And Thomas thought: "swit swoo swan!"
The moment Thomas saw Henry he was quackers for him.

Thomas asked Henry on a date almost immediately.
They couldn't go to the cinema.
Or bowling.
Or to a romantic restaurant.
So, they had to think outside the pond.
Or rather inside it.

They found a discreet spot amongst the bulrushes and nibbled on molluscs and tadpoles.
And they both drank from a giant pitcher of freshwater.
Okay. The Lake.
They both drank from the lake that they were sat on.
It's a bit gross if you think about it too much.

But ultimately: so romantic.

And soon the two boys were goose stepping out together every chance they got.

The lake locals were buzzing with gossip.
Father goose was apoplectic.
Not only was his son dating another person's son.
But the son of the other person was a swan and not a goose.
Mother goose couldn't see the problem. She was just happy that her son finally seemed to be happy.

"But what about the children?" asked the father goose. "Will they be swans or will they be geese, I wander?"
"Well," said his wife, "I suppose they'll be trans-gander."
And that was that.

Now we're into the 90s.
The whole lake was rocking out to the sounds of New Swans on the Block, Koizone and Rage Against the Marine.
And amongst all the rocking no one thought Thomas and Henry were a strange couple anymore.
In fact, everyone wanted to be friends with them.
Everyone was desperate for an invite to their annual fish supper (to be fair, the fish weren't so keen.)
And if you received a bunch of pondweed from them on your birthday you knew you were inner-circle.
Oh, they ran that lake.

But one thing was missing from their lives.
The one thing that would give them the ultimate feeling of fulfilment.
Goslings.

One morning Thomas woke up and found Henry had flown the nest.
Thomas looked across the pond and saw Henry making waves with Henrietta. Another swan.
A few weeks later Thomas saw Henrietta laying eggs.
And a month or so after that he saw the new couple swimming around the lake with their very own family.

He saw there and then why Henry had left.
And he did the bravest thing he had maybe ever done.
He went and joined them.
And the couple became a thruple and brought up the children together.

The lake was beyond caring now.
They had learnt from Thomas and Henry that how you chose to live your life wasn't anybody else's business.
But the humans that lived nearby were fascinated.
They couldn't believe what they were seeing.
And the whole town became obsessed with these three geese living and loving freely and without judgement.

And they lived that way until the noughties.
Of course, no one was rocking out by then, because the music had become truly terrible.
But it didn't matter.
Henry, Henrietta and Thomas had become local celebrities, all because they had made their own kind music.

And played by their own rules.
And taught us one valuable lesson:

Love is love.

The Fairies Fran and Vera: You're All Welcome Here
by Sophia Pollero-Payne, age 7, from Maidstone, UK

THE FAIRIES FRAN AND VERA: YOU'RE ALL WELCOME HERE

✷ ✷ ✷

Fairy Land is (and this will come as no surprise),
The very land where fairies live their very fulfilling lives.

One such fairy is Fabulous Fran. I don't suppose you've met her?
She oozes glitter and magic, alright! She's fairy to the letter.

She lives in a bower with a dour friend who goes by the name of Vera.
In fact, Vile Vera is what she's called and I'd suggest you don't go near her.

Vera has a different approach to life in Fairy Land.
Instead of joy and magic she has misery at hand.

So, give her a wide berth I would, and let Fabulous Fran be your friend.
At least with Fran you know this story should have a happy end.

"Tut, tut, tut," said Vera. "Oh, no, no, no, no," she was uttering.
Reading the *Daily Fairygraph* had really got her muttering.

"Put that down and have some brekkie," said Fran. "You'll feel much better for some porridge."
"I'm not in the mood for food; this newspaper has made me feel horrid.

"Have you read this headline?" snarled Vera, selflessly holding back a sob.
"They'll have us on the breadlines giving that Elf lot all the jobs."

Fran shook her head and clenched her fists to hide her agitation,
For she knew exactly what was coming: Vera's righteous indignation.

And as if on cue Vera stood up and said with placard in tow:
"I'm going to Fairy Towers, to protest against the elves."
To which Fran said a simple: "No."

With a wave of her wand Fran sat Vera back down and tore her placard in two.
"Have you ever wondered why the elves want to come here? Well, tell me Vera: have you?"

"No," said Vera looking resigned as Fran climbed up on her high horse.
(In Fairy Land not just a saying; but a steed you need for discourse.)

"Father Christmas has his elves work every day of the year.
"All for nearly no pay and there's no way he lets them share our Christmas cheer.

"How would you like it if that was your life? Would you look for something better?"
Vera knew Fran was right and rolled her eyes. A visual "ooh, get her."

"And they're not going to take our jobs, they're going to work where they're needed.
"So, I say to every elf: 'You're welcome to Fairy Land unimpeded.' "

Vera forced a loud applause that caused the horse to whinny.
Fran fell to the floor.
"At last!" Vera thought, "I've made her look a ninny!"

As Fabulous Fran regained her poise and became fabulous once more,
They were both surprised to hear a noise. Someone was banging at the door.

The knock was naughty and followed by laughter. Someone was having fun.
"Do it again!" The fairies heard. Could there be more than one?

Knock, laughter, knock, laughter, this went on for a pretty minute.

"Will someone please just let us in?"
"First," said Vera. "Who is it?"

"It's Silly Billy!"
Fran smiled. "Oh, Vile Vera do let's let him in."
She went to the door and there she saw Billy and his friend, the Goblin.

Vera screamed: "Get that thing out of my sight; they're an absolute disgrace."
She started to pace and from her wand sparks hit the goblin's face.

Sparks were flying. The goblin was crying, trying not to get hit on the bum.
"What's all this? This is making me wish, I'd decided not to come!"

Vile Vera earnt her nameand the bower was in disarray.
All because she had let her hate let common sense get knocked away.

"What's your problem? What's a goblin ever done to you?" asked Fran.
"Nothing yet, but you can bet, they should be got rid of if you can.

"You know what they're like, *The Daily Fairygraph* tells you: goblins start wars and all sorts."
"So, you're sure we're all like that?" asked the goblin. "When we're mostly just good sports.

"And besides, you attacked me for no reason I can see,
"Apart from believing what somebody else wants you to believe about me."

Vera had never thought about it like that. Could it be she was wrong?
Even she was beginning to see that stories could have two sides all along.

Fran looked around, the place was a mess and they'd not had breakfast yet!
"Well Vera: you've learnt two lessons already today and you've not even buttered your baguette!"

Now, adventures like these tend to come in threes, so you'll venture

we're due one more.
And would you believe it: it happened the minute they stepped outside
their door.

The group stumbled upon an elderly sprite who was a little down on his
luck.
"Serves him right," declared Vera contritely.
The sprite replied: "Have a heart, duck."

Then with a click of his fingers and before their very eyes,
The sprite turned Vera into an actual duck and no one was surprised.

"She had that coming," said Fran. Billy and the goblin had to agree.
"Well," piped up the sprite, "I'm tired of fairies trying to belittle me.

"After all, I'm a kind of fairy too.
"Just not the same kind of fairy as the two of you.

"My mum and dad left Sprite Town looking for a better life,
"And I was born in Fairy Land, free from Sprite Town strife.

"I grew up here, I know nothing else, so I was upset to find,
"The Fairy Council in Fairy Tower are trying to get rid of my kind.

"They want me gone, I have no choice."
"There must be something you can do?"
"I have nothing to say that I can stay so I have no voice like all of you."

"We must do something," said Fran, "This is a load of twaddle."
But Vera walked away with an angry quack (and she'd picked up quite
a waddle!)

They all followed Vera, letting her guide, which was silly when you
think.
Ducks can float on water but the rest of them would sink.

Vile Vera paddled along, stopping for things to chew.
"You can't be that hungry," said Fran, "I wish I knew what you were up
to!"

Tired, bedraggled, forlorn and wet, they arrived before a tower.

Not the one where Rapunzel lives, but the Fairy seat of power.

They looked up at Fairy Tower and wondered what to do.
But before they knew it, Vera flew up it and then began to poo.

It went everywhere and covered the tower and really began to smell.
"Quick!" said Fran, "we need a trick: a duck to fairy spell."

She waved her wand and with a little glitter Vera went from fowl to fairy.
Vera looked confused and then amused; then they all laughed and got quite lairy.

They stopped and watched the Fairy Council fly away all covered in muck.
"I don't know what their problem is," said Fran, "in some places that's good luck."

"I did that for every elf, goblin and sprite," said Vera. "To send this message clear:
"Fairy Land is a wonderful place and you're all very welcome here!"

"But why? We thought you hated us," said the goblin and sprite.
"I did, but now I see: I really wasn't right.

"I'm lucky to live in a land where everyone can be free,
"And if you're happy, I'm happy. Isn't that how it should be?

The group smiled, Fran forced a hug and gave them all a squeeze.
"The world really is a better place when you've got friends like these!"

The Dream of a King
by Belle Kumble-Rose, age 11 from Lichfield, UK

THE DREAM OF A KING

✳ ✳ ✳

Do you have a dream?
I do.
In fact, I have lots.

I dream that one day that handsome man off the telly is going to turn up at my front door with a big bag of money and a big diamond ring and say "Mama G, will you spend the rest of your life with me?!"

Or there's the dream where instead of water, ice cream comes out of my taps and I shower in ice cream and bath in ice cream and drink ice cream and boil carrots in ice cream and, well, you get the picture.
I like ice cream.

What do you dream about?

…?

I'm still here. Don't worry. Nothing's broken. I'm listening to your answer. Sorry to interrupt. Carry on.

Hu-uh.

Yes.

Lovely.

What amazing dreams you have.

And do you know the most amazing thing about dreams?
If you really believe in them and you really want them: they can come true.

Do you know how I know?
Because that handsome man off the telly has just turned up at my front door and…no, I'm joking. Sadly.

The reason I know that dreams come true is because a very famous man called Martin Luther King Junior once very famously said:

"I have a dream."

And the things he said he dreamed about have all happened.

But it wasn't easy for him.

Martin was born in a city called Atlanta in 1929.
Atlanta is in one of America's Southern states, Georgia.
And at that time life wasn't very easy for black people in that part of America.

And Martin Luther King Jnr was black.

Black people weren't allowed to use the same toilets, hospitals, phone booths or lifts as white people.
And when they went to the theatre or cinema they had to sit at the back so that white people could have the best seats.
Can you imagine that?

When he was little, Martin's best friend was the son of the white family next door.
Both families loved that the boys would play together and were such good friends.
But when they got old enough Martin had to go to a school for black children and his friend had to go to a school for white children.
And they weren't allowed to play together anymore.
Even though they lived next door.
Can you imagine that?

Martin was very clever and did very well in school.

One thing he was very good at was speaking out loud in front of his class.

When he was thirteen Martin won first place in a competition for speaking in front of people.

This was an incredible achievement.

But on the bus on the way home Martin and his teacher got asked to stand up so that a white person could sit down.

Martin said "no" and his teacher had to remind him that it was the law. He had no choice.

A long time after this happened Martin told someone that it had made him the angriest he had ever been in his life.

Can you imagine that?

When Martin was at college he fell in love with a German lady. She was white.

They wanted to get married.

But Martin's friends told him that a black man and a white woman getting married would cause too many problems.

So they decided to just be friends.

Can you imagine that?

Instead, in 1953 Martin married a woman called Coretta.

They had four children.

Martin wanted Coretta to stay at home and bring up the children.

But she was like him.

So, she said "no" and joined his crusade to make the world fair for everyone.

Gradually Martin started to become famous for getting involved with lots of causes that would make the world better.

But he faced a lot of challenges.

In 1955, He stood up for other black people when they refused to give their seat to a white person on a bus, in Montgomery, Alabama.

People got so upset with him that they tried to blow up his house.

Can you imagine that?

In 1963 Martin was involved in a March on Washington.

Lots of black people marched with him to ask the American President to change the laws so that black people could use the same things as white people.

And so that black people could get paid the same as white people, as well.

It was here that Martin Luther King gave a speech and said:

"I have a dream."

It was here that people realised how important his beliefs were going to be for the future of the world.

Change does not happen quickly.

You have to really work for it.

In 1965 Martin led another march. This time from Selma, Alabama; because black people still weren't getting the same rights as white people.

This made a lot of people angry and a lot of Martin's friends got hurt.

Just because they were asking to be treated the same as everybody else.

Can you imagine that?

Some people got very angry at Martin himself.

And in 1968 in a motel in Tennessee a man shot Martin with a gun.

Some people thought the man had done the right thing.

But most people were upset and the President decided that the whole country should mourn the loss of Martin Luther King Junior.

This is a sad story.

Sorry about that.

I should have warned you.

But a lot of good things have happened because of Martin's work.

You can go to school with people who have any colour skin.

You and your friends can sit together at the cinema and on the bus.

Everyone has the right to the same minimum wage; no matter who they are.

And everyone knows that this is right.
And everyone knows that this is fair.

So next time you think:

"I have a dream."

Follow that dream.
Because you might just change the world.

THE TROLL HUNTY

* * *

The troll was getting ready for a big night out.
There was a big goblet of Berry Juice on the bureau.
There were party tunes banging out around the forest.
And there was the outfit of all outfits hanging by the massive bed.
This troll was going to turn heads tonight.

They touched up their lipstick.
Tweaked their lovely blonde curls.
Slipped into their favourite pink sequin dress.
Chose the perfect handbag.
Blew themselves a kiss in the mirror.
And waltzed out the door.

It was going to be the perfect night.
In fact, it already was.
The sun was setting.
The air was warm.
And the birds were singing their goodnight songs.
The troll took a deep breath.
Twirled their skirt.
And skipped towards town.

Now, trolls come from Norway.
But, unless it's Oslo I can't say Norwegian names.
So let's assume the troll was going anywhere in the world that it

wanted.
Like Birmingham.
Let's say the troll was going to Birmingham.

And the troll was looking fiiiiiiine tonight.
As they skipped their way through the forest they couldn't help getting the attention of other trolls.

"Oi, oi! How you doin', darlin'? Looking good, Terence!"

Terence rolled his mascaraed eyes. "I've told you boys before, it's Stacey when I'm dressed like this."

They wolf-whistled and watched Stacey walk away towards the town.
And as soon as Stacey was out of sight they laughed, loudly and for a long time.
Stacey couldn't see them, but she could hear them.
"I suppose they're all going to talk about me now," she thought.
But just like Taylor Swift would do, Stacey shook it off and kept walking.

As far as Terence was concerned, what he did was his own business.
And becoming Stacey was the only way he could fulfil his dream of being near humans, without causing a disturbance.

The first time he had gone into Birmingham, as we're calling it, with his dungarees on and club in is hand he had caused quite the disturbance.
People had run from Terence in terror.
I mean, he is really big.
You would probably run too.

But then he'd seen two of his troll girlfriends, Trixie and Tyra, just doing their weekly shop.
And rather than running away the locals wanted to talk to them.
And the children wanted to play with them.
That gave Terence an idea.
And the following week he went back into town with a wig, false eyelashes and a new name.
He told his new friends he was a female bodybuilder.

And they all went dancing.
That was that.

And Tracey was on her way to meet her friends now.
Except as she walked through the forest she noticed something strange.
He saw a group of four humans in a Land Rover.
Driving towards where he had just come from.
They were all holding big strips that looked like lights.
Light sabres, I suppose.
But this isn't Star Wars.
It's probably better, no?
#joking

Bright light isn't good for a Troll.
They tend to turn to stone if it is shone at them.
That's why most of Norway's best statues are really big and look really scared.

"This doesn't look right," said Terence, to nobody in particular.

But Tracey kept walking.
If the other trolls were going to laugh at what she chose to wear, well, then maybe they deserved to get turned to stone.
Those Troll Hunters could have the mean trolls.

But as she kept walking she started to hear deep screams.
Then the sound of stone forming.
And then maniacal human laughter.

Scream.
Stone.
Laugh.

Scream.
Stone.
Laugh.

Scream.
Stone.

Laugh.

Tracey couldn't take it.
Neither could Terence.
And their one troll body turned around and ran back home.
Back to where the noises were coming from.

When Terence got back he saw a scene of devastation.
Trolls had clearly been running every which way.
Homes were flattened.
Dense patches of trees now had troll shaped clearings in them.
And where beautiful flowers had been there now stood stone trolls.
It looked like a troll museum.

Tracey could see strips of light being waved around.
So, she took a deep breath.
Pulled the fringe of her wig down over her eyes.
And stepped towards the Troll Hunters.

The minute they saw her they stopped.
"Sorry love, we didn't realise there were any lady trolls around."

"How am I different to the man trolls?" asked Tracey.

"Oh you're not, it's just, er, not nice to be violent around ladies is it, because you can't defend yourselves."

Now there's someone that's never been to Birmingham.

Terence saw his chance.
He bent down and scooped the Troll Hunters up so they were all in his one hand.
He brought them up to his eye and said:

"You don't think a lady can defend herself?"

"No," they all answered, nervously.

"Well, you came to the wrong lady!"

And with that Tracey threw the Troll Hunters as high and as far as she could.

Which as you can imagine, is very high and very far.
She heard their screams get quieter the further away they got.
And as she heard the last one land in the sea she smiled, picked up her handbag, adjusted her wig and got ready to head back into town.

But she was stopped by the sound of slow handclapping.
And a circle of relieved looking trolls.

"Well, well, well, Tracey. We didn't think you had it in you."

"Didn't have it in me?" Tracey laughed. "Didn't have it in me?
"You think I can put up with all of you laughing at me because of how I choose to live my life.
"You think I can put up with all the name calling.
"You think I can put up with being made to feel inferior to everyone.
"And yet, after all that, you don't think I'd have the strength to deal with some tiny humans waving torches around.
"Give me strength.
"In fact, don't; because I don't need it.
"I'm stronger than the lot of you.
"It takes a lot of guts and a lot of courage to live my life this way and don't you forget it!"

It was a very rousing speech.
In fact, Terence had started to notice that his mascara was running.
And because of that he'd failed to notice that all the trolls had gone away.
And returned.
Wearing wigs, flowers, dresses, make-up, glitter, eyelashes, heels.
And Trixie and Tyra had turned up with Tracey's human friends from the town who now saw Tracey for who Terence was.
And they loved that Tracey could be who she was with them, finally.

One of the trolls stepped forward.
"Oi, oi! You saved the day today. And so we're going to have a party. To celebrate you. Both of you.
"No tea, no shade, but you are bringing the house down. I am gagging on your Daytime Human Eleganza; you are feeling the fantasy and it is

giving me life!
"And it takes a real strong troll, to be THAT troll, hunty."

And with that the Trolls and the humans had a ball.
Category is: You Do You.
(And it will always work out for the best, hunty.)

When Eunice Upon a Star
by Alice New, age 8, from Southampton, UK

WHEN EUNICE UPON A STAR

✳ ✳ ✳

Have you ever heard of anyone who didn't like Christmas?

No, me neither.

But at the Happy Hill Farm:
The pigs,
The cows,
The sheep,
The chickens,
The goats,
The horses
And especially the turkeys,
They all detested Christmas.

In fact, there was only one animal in the whole farmyard who agreed with you and I:
Eunice the Unicorn.
She loved Christmas.
And every Christmas she wished she could be anywhere other than the Happy Hill Farm.

Every year, Eunice the Unicorn would watch the farm next door put up a beautiful Christmas Tree.
But the Happy Hill Farm would stay bare.

Every year, Eunice the Unicorn would watch the farm next door put up beautiful, bright Christmas lights.

But the Happy Hill Farm would stay dark.

Every year, Eunice the Unicorn would watch the farm next door dancing and singing to beautiful Christmas songs.
But the Happy Hill Farm would stay quiet.

Would that make you sad?
It would make me sad.
And it made Eunice sad.
Very, very sad.

One day, Eunice's best friend Hortense the Horse had had enough.
Eunice was a Unicorn after all.
And unicorns are meant to have a fabulous time.
All the time.
It's unicorn law.

"Eunice!" said Hortense. "I think it's time you found out why nobody else on this farm likes Christmas."
"But what would be the point? They've never liked Christmas," neighed Eunice.
"Maybe you can change that!"
"Do you think so?"
"I think you can do anything."
(Hortense was a very good best friend!)

So, Eunice the Unicorn took a leap of faith and flew over her fence.
And Hortense the Horse took a running jump and jumped over her fence.
They had barely landed when Hortense saw her best friend trotting off to start her investigations.

"Excuse me," said Eunice. "Mr Pig?"
"What do you want?"
"I want to know why you don't like Christmas."
"Christmas is cold, it is. And we don't get given no blankets; but every Christmas the big people in that farmhouse have something for their dinner called Pigs in Blankets.
"How do you think that makes us feel?"

"I never thought about that," said Eunice.

"So, what would make you like Christmas?" asked Hortense.
"Blankets!" said Mr Pig.
"Ah, to feel loved!" realised Eunice.

Hortense took her friend to the next field.

"Excuse me," said Eunice. "Mrs Cow?"
"What do you want?"
"I want to know why you don't like Christmas."
"Every year the children in the village put on a Nativity play. And there are sheep in it and donkeys too, but never cows.
"How do you think that makes us feel?"

"I never thought about that," said Eunice.

"So, what would make you like Christmas?" asked Hortense.
"To be in the play!" said Mrs Cow.
"Ah, to feel included!" realised Eunice.

Hortense took her friend to the next field.

"Excuse me," said Eunice. "Mr Sheep?"
"What do you want?"
"I want to know why you don't like Christmas."
"Everyone gets to dress up at Christmas and look amazing, but we just get to wear the same old woolly jumpers and look like we always do.
"How do you think that makes us feel?"

"I never thought about that," said Eunice.

"So, what would make you like Christmas?" asked Hortense.
"To look as magical as a unicorn." said Mr Sheep.
"Ah, to feel special!" realised Eunice.

That night Eunice cried herself to sleep.
How could she make everyone feel loved?
And included?
And special?

She was only one unicorn.
And her magic could only stretch so far.

That night the sky shone with thousands of stars.
That night Eunice wished harder than she had ever wished that she could help all of her friends.
That night every star answered Eunice's wish.
And that night every star turned into a unicorn.

When Eunice woke up.
When Hortense woke up.
When the rest of the farm woke up.
They got the shock of their lives.

Everywhere they looked there were unicorns.
Magical unicorns.
Glittery unicorns.
Rainbow unicorns.
And unicorn unicorns.
(Some unicorns are actually quite low key!)

"What's going on?" whinnied Hortense.
"I thought I was seeing double,
"But now I see I'm seeing thousands-able."

"What IS going on?" wondered Eunice.

The most majestic of all the unicorns stepped forward.
"You wished upon a star, Eunice.
"And now we're here to help you restore Christmas spirit to Happy Hill Farm!"

And so they did.

A group of unicorns flew as fast as they could and collected all the ivy and Christmas tree needles they could find.
When they got back Eunice helped them sew the ivy together using the Christmas tree needles they had collected.
They were making blankets.
More blankets than you have ever seen.

"Wow!" thought Hortense.

Another group of unicorns flew around the farm and picked up as many haybales as they could carry.
They brought them to an empty field and Eunice helped them push the haybales together.
They were making a stage.
The biggest stage you have ever seen.
"Wow!" thought Hortense.

Some of the younger unicorns chased each other around, collecting berries and acorns and pine cones and milk bottle caps and anything that sparkled.
When they had tired themselves out Eunice showed them how to turn their finds into necklaces and baubles and tinsel.
They were making decorations.
The most beautiful decorations you have ever seen.
"Wow!" thought Hortense.

The unicorns worked tirelessly.
And before Eunice knew it: Happy Hill Farm was ready.
Ready to love Christmas again.

The rest of the farm animals wandered into the field.
Cautious and nervous.
What had been happening?
What was about to happen?

Then the unicorns threw glitter up in the air and the field magically lit up with real fairies illuminating the trees.

Everyone got given a blanket.
To stay warm.
And because they were loved.

The cows got to go on stage and tell jokes and sing songs.
And the rest of the farm laughed and sang along.
Then they let everyone join them on stage.
Because everyone was included.

And the sheep got dressed up in the most fabulous decorations.
They were the talk of the field.
They felt so special.
And so did everyone else.

Everyone was having the time of their lives!

"Well," said Mr Pig. "Thanks to Eunice, I think I might just love Christmas again."
"So do I," said Mrs Cow.
"So do I," said Mr Sheep.
"So do I," said everyone.

And what about you?
Do you love Christmas?
I hope so!
Because I know one thing for certain:

You are loved.
You are included.
And you are special.

Merry Christmas.

YOU BETTER TWERK

* * *

"Twerk is a verb.
"A verb is a word that means you are doing something.
"But what are you doing when you twerk?"

"Miss!"

"Yes, Whitney?"

"Is it what people from Yorkshire say when they're going to their job?"

"No, Whitney. People from Yorkshire go t'werk."

"Miss!"

"Yes, Janet?"

"Is it what my mum calls my brother?"

"No, Janet. Your mum calls your brother a twerp."

"Miss!"

"Yes, Michael?"

"Is it what I do when I dance?"

Meet Michael.
Michael likes to twerk.
In fact, Michael likes to do any dance.
He likes to do the Floss.

He likes to do the Worm.
He likes to do the Robot.
But most of all, Michael likes to twerk

Do you know how to twerk?
Here's how:

Stand with your feet apart, parallel to your shoulders, but with your knees behind your toes. Bend into a squatting position, placing your hands upon your knees and turning your feet out; this will help you keep your balance and perform the manoeuvre with grace and style. Keep your upper body straight, face forward and then move your hips back and forth. If you're a beginner start slowly and then you can gradually pick up the pace. Something by Beyoncé or Shakira usually helps you get in the mood. And finally: it should look like your bottom is going up and down. That's it. You've got it.

And Michael got it too.
But a lot of people wished he didn't get it.
Like his teacher.

Michael was just about to get on his desk at school to demonstrate the twerk when Miss Jackson said:

"You better NOT twerk."

Michael stopped.
"I'm sorry, Miss Jackson."

When Michael's mum, Eileen, told him that dinner was ready, he got so excited he couldn't do anything else but twerk.

"You better NOT twerk."

Michael stopped.
"Oh, come on, Eileen."

When Michael was helping his dad put up some shelves, he used the power of his twerk to bang a nail into the wall.

"What have I told you, Michael? We have to play safe around this equipment, so...

You better NOT twerk."

Michael stopped.
"Papa, don't preach."

All Michael heard all day and every day was.

"You better NOT twerk."

But what nobody ever told him was why not.
It was what he was good at.
It was what made him happy.
It was what made him different to everybody else.
Michael needed to find a way to show everyone that twerking is what made Michael Michael!

Can you guess what happens next?

It was a chilly evening.
Michael and his friend Mariah were on their way to the Village Green.
It was Bonfire Night.
The whole village loved Bonfire Night.
Excited families were rushing past them with sparklers and toffee apples.
Couples were holding hands and were all wrapped up in scarves and hats.
All around them Michael and Mariah could hear laughter and cheering and excitement.

But when they got to the Village Green all the laughter and cheering stopped.
Where was the bonfire?
Everyone was looking around confused.
Michael looked at Mariah.
Mariah looked at Michael.
"Huh?"

They could see the pile of wood.
And they could see people trying to set the pile of wood alight.
But they couldn't see any fire.

The Mayor got up to make an announcement.
"It is with great regret that I announce Bonfire Night is cancelled."

Everyone sighed a disappointed sigh.

"We just can't keep the fire going, we need something to fan it with."

People started to search through their pockets.
Some tissues? No!
A marble? No!
A receipt from the petrol station? Double no!

Mariah looked at Michael.
Michael looked at Mariah.
And then Michael put his hand up.
"Please, I think I might be able to do something to help."

Everyone gasped.
Everyone knew what Michael meant.
Everyone looked at the Mayor.
Everyone looked at Michael.
Everyone looked back at the Mayor.

Silence.

Then.

"Michael, I have one thing to say to you:

"YOU BETTER TWERK!"

Michael skipped over to the bonfire and twerked like he had never twerked before.
And as his bottom went up and down, flames to started to grow on the bonfire.
And as his bottom fanned the flames, the flames started to go higher and higher!

It was working!

Soon Mariah joined in.
And then the Mayor.
Then Miss Jackson.
Then Eileen.
Then Papa.

The whole village was twerking.
The whole village was fanning the flames with their bottoms.
And before they knew it the Village Green was glowing with the biggest bonfire anyone had ever seen.

People were cheering again, but this time for Michael.
Because of Michael, Bonfire Night had been saved.

Michael went on to do great things.
He taught twerking in schools.
He started a new fitness phenomenon called 'Twerk to Twenty'.
(No one knew if it worked – but they gave him money for it anyway.)
And he was the first Olympic athlete to win a gold medal for twerking.
He was a national hero.

All because he followed his heart.
All because he was true to himself.
All because he never let anyone tell him that who he was was wrong.

And you?

YOU BETTER TWERK!

Or even better:

YOU BETTER BE YOU!

ABOUT THE AUTHOR

❋ ❋ ❋

MAMA G

Mama G is a pantomime dame who tells stories about being who you are and loving who you want. She has visited theatres, libraries, bookshops, museums and festivals all over the UK and has even appeared in Canada (live on stage) and in America (on screen.)

If you want to find out more about Mama G, or have any questions for her head to her Facebook page:

www.facebook.com/MamaGStories

ROBERT PEARCE

Robert Pearce is a professional actor and pantomime dame in the UK. He trained at Rose Bruford College and SFA University in Texas. He has appeared in over 25 pantomimes, as well as writing and directing productions all over the country.

When not in panto, Robert has toured the UK in musicals, murder mysteries and stage versions of popular children's TV shows. In London he's appeared in productions of Shakespeare, Checkhov and sketch shows.

Visit www.robertpearceactor.com to keep up to date!

PETITE PANTOS

Petite Pantos are a British theatre company who specialise in producing pantomimes with a social conscience and in unusual or unexpected locations.

Previous productions have included: *Two Petite Pantos*, *Mother Goose*, *Now That's What I Call Panto*, *The Pirates of Panto* and *Dick Whittington*; taking them to venues such as theatres, old cinemas, storage containers and Victorian pubs!

"Petite Pantos with the hearts and souls of giants!" - London Pub Theatres.

For more info visit www.petitepantos.com or www.facebook.com/petitepantos

Printed in Poland
by Amazon Fulfillment
Poland Sp. z o.o., Wrocław